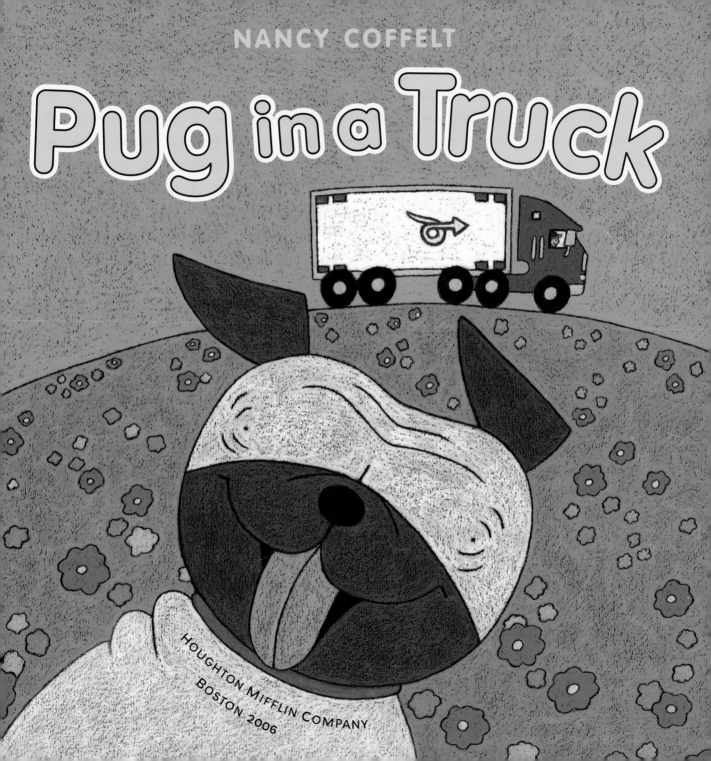

This is our truck.
It's flat in the front.

This is me.
My nose is as
flat as the front
of our truck.

This is my friend.

He calls me Pug.
I'm Pug in a truck!

This is where we pick up our load to deliver.

When we hook up the trailer, our truck's not a bobtail anymore. Sometimes we haul goods for stores to sell. Sometimes we haul food that farmers have grown.

Sniff, sniff.

No food in this cargo!

My friend lifts me into the cab.

RUMBLE, RUMBLE.

The diesel engine growls.

GRUMBLE, GRUMBLE.

So do I.

Bow-wow!

We have a load
to deliver!

We get on the
freeway and put
the hammer down.

Now we're
heading straight
out of the city.

We see lots of other
vehicles on the road. Look —

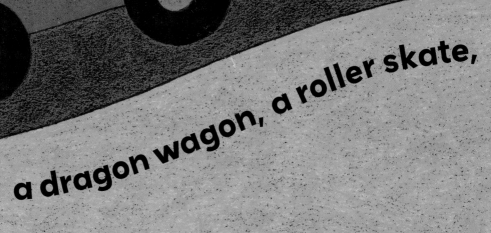

a dragon wagon, a roller skate,

a four-wheeler, and a skateboard!

But I'm always on
the lookout for big
rigs like ours.

Finally, I see an eighteen-wheeler hauling a load of toothpicks.

Look at me! I'm as tough as your truck.

HONK - HONK
goes the driver.

Bow-wow,
I'm as loud as
your horn!

Badadadada!

Our air brakes bark.

Bow-wow!

So do I.

Ground clouds —
my friend can't see the road!

We switch on our fog lights.
"Pug, only five more yardsticks until
we're over the pass and in the clear."

Bow-wow, everybody follow us!
Our fog lights lead the way.
So do my barks.

Crackle goes the CB.

"You got your ears on? Thanks, barking buddy. You helped everyone keep the shiny side up and the greasy side down."

Now we're at double nickel again and back in business. But all that barking has

tired

me

out.

When I wake up it's dark.
The headlights look like
stars on the highway.

Where are we?

Bow-wow,
truck stop!

We can fuel up
here.

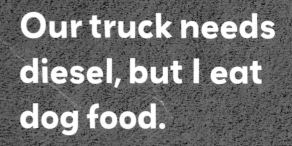

Our truck needs
diesel, but I eat
dog food.

My friend needs to fuel up too.
But no pugs allowed in the restaurant.

After dinner we take a walk around the truck stop.

There drivers can get their hair cut or their shoes shined. They can buy snacks or maps. And some drivers are here to park their trucks and get some sleep. **Bow-wow**, it's our bedtime too.

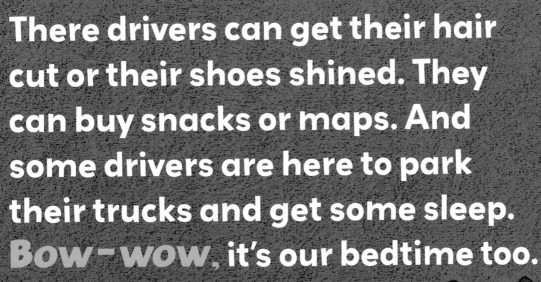

This is our bed,
behind the cab.

It's soft and warm
and we need to rest.

Because tomorrow we're back on the road.

I'm Pug in a truck, and we have a load to deliver!

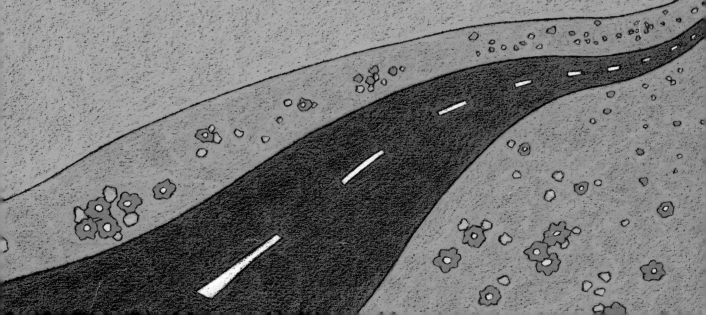

TRUCKER GLOSSARY

Bobtail
a truck running without a trailer.

Double nickel
fifty-five miles per hour, the speed limit.

Dragon wagon
a tow truck.

Eighteen-wheeler
any articulated truck (even though many have fewer or more than eighteen wheels).

Four-wheeler
a passenger car.

Got your ears on?
an expression used when looking for someone on the CB. ("Hey, HT, you got your ears on?")

Ground clouds
fog

Hammer down
to go fast, step on it.

Keeping the shiny side up and the greasy side down
driving safely, avoiding an accident.

Roller skate
any small car. Originally referred to a Volkswagen.

Skateboard
a flatbed trailer.

Toothpicks
a load of lumber.

Yardstick
a mile marker alongside a highway.

For Dutch, Maggie, Chip, Belle, Fred, Judy, Pooh, Chloe, and Ollie, our four-legged family members

www.houghtonmifflinbooks.com
The text of this book is set in Grenadine bold.
ISBN-13:978-0618-56319-7
Printed in Singapore
TWP 10 9 8 7 6 5 4 3 2 1

Library of Congress Cataloging-in-Publication Data
Coffelt, Nancy.
   Pug in a truck/written and illustrated by Nancy Coffelt.
   p. cm.
   Summary: A pug dog describes his life with his human friend as they make a living by hauling loads in an eighteen-wheeler truck. Includes glossary of trucking terms.
   ISBN 0-618-56319-9 (hardcover)
   [1. Pug—Fiction. 2. Truck driving—Fiction. 3. Dogs—Fiction.] I. Title.
PZ7.C658Pug 2006
[E]—dc22
                                          2005025444